Leo the Late Bloomer

BY ROBERT KRAUS • PICTURES BY JOSE ARUEGO

Windmill Books

New York

Leo the Late Bloomer
Text copyright © 1971 by Robert Kraus
Illustrations copyright © 1971 by José Aruego

LC Number 70-159154
ISBN 0-87807-042-7
ISBN 0-87807-043-5 (lib. bdg.)
ISBN 0-06-443348-X (pbk.)

'Windmill Books' and the colophon
accompanying it are a trademark of
Windmill Books, Inc., registered in
the United States Patent Office.
Published by Windmill Books, Inc.
Distributed by HarperCollins Publishers.

For Ken Dewey

J. A.

For Pamela, Bruce
and Billy

R. K.

Leo couldn't do anything right.

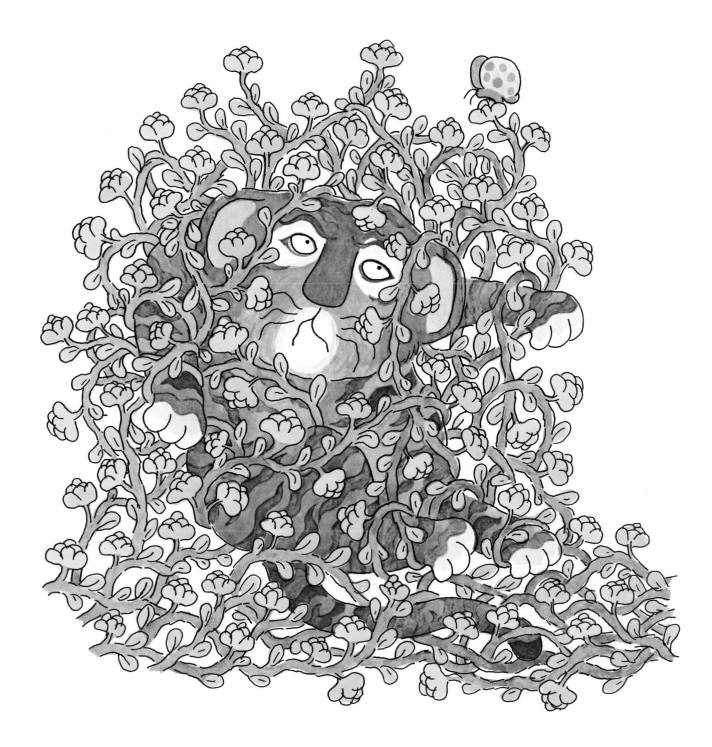

He couldn't read.

He couldn't write.

He couldn't draw.

He was a sloppy eater.

And, he never said a word.

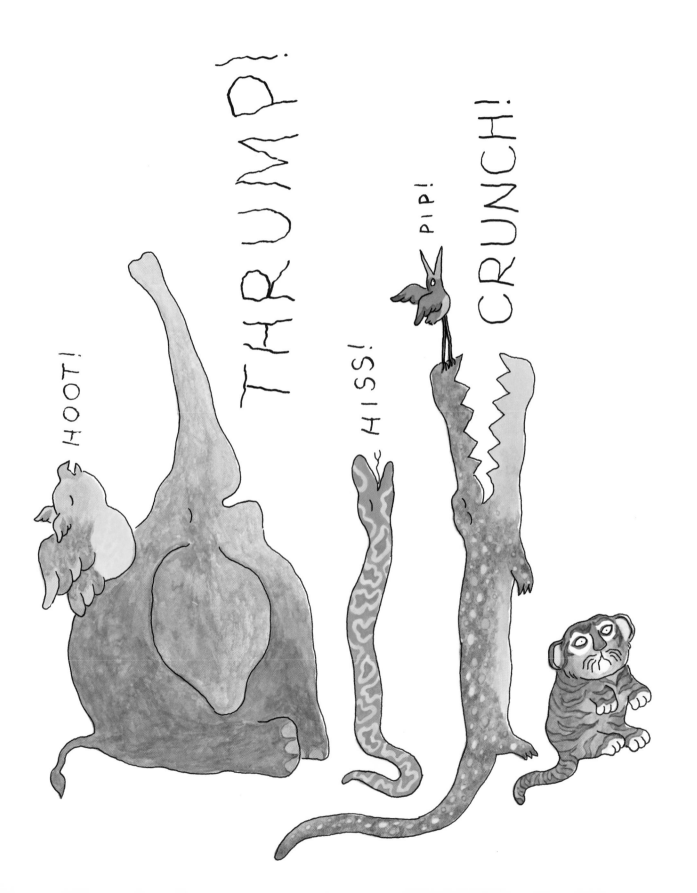

"What's the matter with Leo?"
asked Leo's father.
"Nothing," said Leo's mother.
"Leo is just a late bloomer."
"Better late than never," thought Leo's father.

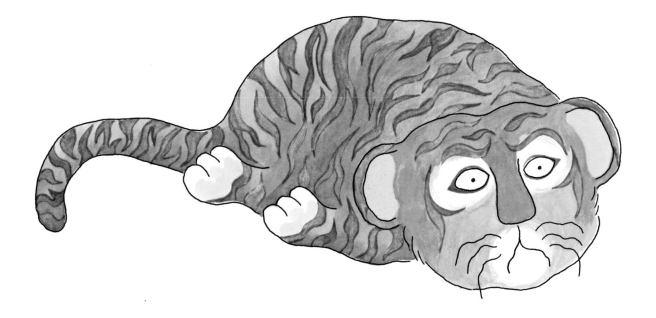

Every day Leo's father watched him
for signs of blooming.

And every night Leo's father watched him for signs of blooming.

"Are you sure Leo's a bloomer?"
asked Leo's father.
"Patience," said Leo's mother.
"A watched bloomer doesn't bloom."

So Leo's father watched television
instead of Leo.

The snows came.
Leo's father wasn't watching.
But Leo still wasn't blooming.

The trees budded.
Leo's father wasn't watching.
But Leo still wasn't blooming.

Then one day,
in his own good time,
Leo bloomed!

He could read !

He could write!

He could draw!

He ate neatly!

He also spoke.
And it wasn't just a word.
It was a whole sentence.
And that sentence was...

"I made it!"